MAGNUM OPUS

CAITLIN MARCEAU

Magnum Opus
by Caitlin Marceau

Magnum Opus is a work of fiction. Names, places, and incidents either are products of the author's imagination or are used fictitiously. Any resemblance to actual events, locales, or persons, living or dead, is entirely coincidental.

All rights reserved. No part of this book may be reproduced in any form or by any electronic or mechanical means, including information storage and retrieval systems, without permission in writing from the publisher, except by reviewers, who may quote brief passages in a review.

Copyright © **2023, Caitlin Marceau**
Published by Timber Ghost Press
Printed in the United States of America
Edited by: Beverly Bernard
Cover Art and Design by: Truborn Design
Interior Design: Timber Ghost Press

www.TimberGhostPress.com

Contents

Dedication	IV
1. January	1
2. February	16
3. March	37
4. April	51
Acknowledgements	56
About the Author	57
A Note from Timber Ghost Press	59

DEDICATION

To Georgia
Thank you for being the Kim to my Charlotte.
I promise I won't murder you.
Probably.

January

"Congratulations!" Kim screams from the front steps of the townhouse, carrying a bottle of pink champagne in one hand and a box of cupcakes tied with glittery ribbon in the other. Her breath frames her face in tendrils of silver as the snow lazily falls onto the concrete around her.

"Thank yoooooou!" Charlotte screams back, wrapping her arms around her friend in a hug before letting go and beckoning the other woman inside.

Kim kicks her boots off onto the shoe rack by the door before stepping out of the entranceway and into the small home. Charlotte takes the pastries and alcohol, bringing them into the kitchen while Kim shrugs off her winter coat and tosses it carelessly onto one of the metal hooks on the wall.

"You must be excited," Kim says, taking a seat at the kitchen island as Charlotte rinses out a set of old champagne flutes. They were a wedding present from her mother that she'd only ever used once before: after signing her divorce papers.

"I am excited! But it's really not that big of a deal. I kind of feel silly celebrating, to be honest," she says, cheeks warm and coloured pink.

"Why would you be embarrassed?"

"I don't know. I just, I guess it's not that big of a deal and we're treating it like one," she lies.

It *is* a big deal and she *is* excited, but she doesn't want to admit this to Kim.

"It's a *huge* deal," Kim argues. "You have a book coming out from a major publisher! What's not to get excited about?"

"I don't know. I mean, it's not like it's my first one. And, let's be honest, it's not like it's going to be as big as yours have been."

Kim waves a hand dismissively. "It's going to be bigger. I can feel it. Besides, it's not like publishing's a competition anyway, right?"

"Right!"

Wrong. It isn't a competition for Kim because she's already won.

Kim Lavoie. *The* Kim Lavoie, a household name when it comes to all things romantic comedy. Her books have made the New York Times Best Seller List, are frequently raved about by middle-aged housewives stuck in monogamous vanilla marriages, and are even in the process of being adapted into a TV series by Netflix (although Kim refuses to confirm the details with anyone, even Charlotte). She writes quirky romances about the joys of domesticity, uplifting stories that could never come true. Despite her background in literature, having studied it in university alongside Charlotte, her writing is designed with entertainment—not literary canon—in mind.

Kim is, to put it bluntly, everything Charlotte dislikes about popular writers today. Not that she'll ever admit that to her friend.

"Do you want any help?"

"No, I've got it," Charlotte says, drying the flutes with a dish towel and setting them down on the island next to the champagne. She takes out two small plates and a stack of napkins and sets them down next to the cupcakes, a smile plastered on her face as she moves about the room. With a pair of scissors, she cuts through the metallic ribbon and opens the white bakery box.

"Don't they look good?" Kim asks.

Amazing, Charlotte says, emphasizing the second syllable of the word and feeling like a sorority girl in the process. "*So* classy looking."

"Right? Totally swanky," Kim laughs, taking one out of the box. It's decorated with millennial pink frosting with white sprinkles, perfectly matching the champagne.

Charlotte grabs one with white swirls of frosting and a dusting of edible silver. She bites into it, revealing a funfetti cake with a strawberry compote centre.

"Delicious," Charlotte says, mouth full.

Kim nods enthusiastically.

"Want me to pop it?" She gestures at the bottle.

"I've got it," Charlotte tells her, twisting off the metal cage covering the top. She places both thumbs under the lip of the cork and pushes upward, turns the bottle, repositions her thumbs, and presses upward again. She repeats the process a few times before the cork dislodges with a loud pop. She pours the alcohol into the crystal glasses, and the two women clink them together in cheers before taking a sip of bubbly pink liquid.

"So, what's the book called?"

"*And All the Rivers Burned,*" Charlotte says proudly.

"Ooh! So dramatic! I love it! And what's it about? I mean, if I can ask?" Kim says, resting her chin on her hand as she leans against the wooden top of the island.

"It's a story about death and divorce. This woman and her husband have lost their son to leukemia and his death drives them apart. So, we see the woman try to navigate both of these losses while discovering herself."

"That sounds amazing... and really heavy. I can't wait to cry my eyes out while I read it."

"Yeah, it's definitely intense," Charlotte admits. "But I really think it's my best book yet. Like, I don't know how to explain it, but it just *feels* like art is supposed to feel. You know?"

"Definitely," Kim says with a smile.

Charlotte grins back at her, trying hard to quiet the envious voice in the back of her brain that doubts the other woman knows what great art is, let alone that she's ever written any. She tries to ignore the part of herself that belittles Kim's books and reduces them to just cheesy romances that capitalize on sex, scandal, and cheap tropes. It's hard to do; Charlotte likes to think her own work has always been *real* art that focuses on what really matters. It examines loss, identity, and womanhood. The things that define us. The things that are important.

Even if those things don't sell quite as many books.

Charlotte takes another sip of her drink.

"And it comes out in April, right?" Kim asks.

"Yeah."

"Oh, this is going to be so exciting! I was really hoping we'd have books out at the same time again."

Charlotte suddenly feels like she's free-falling, as though the floor has opened up beneath her.

"What?"

"Well," Kim says sheepishly, "that is part of what I came here to celebrate. They moved the release date of my next book to April, right in time for Mother's Day! Although, I'm not really sure *why* they're moving it; this isn't a romance like my other books. It's more of a murder mystery with elements of—"

"Your book is coming out in April too," Charlotte interrupts, throat tight. It's not a question.

"Yeah! Our books are going to be coming out at the same time!"

"Yay!" Charlotte forces out before draining the rest of her drink.

Her heart thunders furiously against her rib cage. She already knows what will happen in a few months: Kim's book will outsell hers. Any praise, any sales, any notoriety she was hoping to get from this new book is dead in the water. Her book will be forgotten and left unread on shelves, or worse, will be doomed to gather dust at the bottom of discount book bins.

Just like the last time.

"I knew you'd be excited!" Kim enthuses.

"Of course I am! Why wouldn't I be?"

Kim shrugs. "I know book releases can be a really personal thing and I didn't want to step on your toes, you know? But like, the books are so different that I can't see it being a problem."

"Obviously," Charlotte grits out. She grabs the bottle of pink champagne and pours more into her own flute before refilling Kim's as well. She lifts her glass, Kim mirroring her, and tilts it back and downs the whole thing. She pours another round from the bottle, Kim shaking her head as her glass is filled to the top.

"Oh, I shouldn't. I'm driving and I'm a *total* lightweight."

"It's just one more drink. I'm sure you'll be fine."

Kim hesitates before lifting the glass to her lips. Charlotte knows she shouldn't pressure her friend to drink, especially when Kim has always had a hard time controlling herself around liquor, but she doesn't care. She's too upset to think clearly.

She downs her own drink again.

"You must really like that champagne," Kim laughs before swallowing hers back too.

"Well, it's a night to celebrate, isn't it? We *both* have books coming out this year, after all. If that isn't a reason to celebrate, I don't know what is."

The plastic smile falls off her face as she turns away from Kim and walks through the doorway to the living room. She grabs a few bottles of heavy liquor from the bar cart and returns to the tiny kitchen to mix some drinks. Kim squirms excitedly in her seat when she sees the tequila, tapping on her cellphone's screen to check the time.

"I guess it's time to party!" Kim yells, clapping her hands with excitement.

"Totally."

By the time Kim gets up from her seat at the table, she's had more drinks than either of them can count. What started off as a few glasses of champagne quickly turned into shots, a couple of mixed drinks, and an entire bottle of wine. Now, Charlotte watches as Kim holds onto the back of a wooden chair for dear life, her legs shaking as she struggles to stand on her own.

Across the table from her, Charlotte messily eats her third cupcake, the buzz from the booze already starting to wear while the depression sets in even harder. She licks the frosting off the top and nibbles at the bottom of the pastry, not noticing—or not caring—that the cream filling is leaking from one of the holes she's made in the base of the cake. She chews with her mouth open and takes small sips of her water, trying to dull the hangover she's already getting.

"Y-you still have wine," Kim says, speech slurred and sluggish as she points. The glass of red rests on the table next to Charlotte, the wine leaving streaks down the thin glass and forming rings on the hardwood table. Charlotte can't begin to worry right now about how she's going to try (and fail) to clean them off.

"Yup," she says, voice gravelly from the alcohol.

Kim flaps her hand, pantomiming for her friend to pass over the rest of the wine. Charlotte rolls her eyes and slides the glass over, her stomach churning as she watches the red liquid slosh against the walls of the glass. Although Kim is finally standing, Charlotte suspects she doesn't actually have the coordination to move anywhere given her level of intoxication. Although Charlotte stopped drinking a few hours ago, the liquor having only numbed her face and not her fury, she's been popping Tylenol and Tums like candy in an attempt to stop the already developing headache and nausea.

Kim picks up the glass and throws the drink back in a single gulp as Charlotte watches, revolted.

"How the fuck are you still going?"

"Huh?" Kim asks, eyes unfocused as she sets the empty stemware down and looks at her friend.

"Never mind."

"What? W-what'd you say?"

"Nothing, Kim. You should sit down. You're going to fall."

"B-ut you'll catch me!" she slurs happily. Her cheeks are rosy and she grins wide like a child, her teeth tinted red from the wine.

"No. You'll fall, hit my floor, and crack your head open. Sit the fuck down," Charlotte tells her flatly.

Kim frowns and looks down at the ground sadly, only half aware of how rudely she's being talked to. Charlotte feels a twinge of guilt at how she's treating her friend, but she's more ashamed that part of her enjoys how cruel she's being. She knows it's not Kim's fault that her book's release was moved up, and she knows that her friend only has the best of intentions, but it doesn't stop her from hating the situation or from hating herself for how jealous she is of Kim.

She adds, "Please, I really don't want to clean blood off of hardwood."

"You're fun-ny," Kim laughs, letting go of the wooden chair and trying her luck at standing on her own. Her legs shake and her body wobbles with each small step that she takes. She makes for the sofa, her eyes struggling to stay open. Charlotte is tempted to stick a leg out as Kim passes her by, but she stops herself, sick with shame that the thought of hurting her friend had even crossed her mind.

"Here," Charlotte huffs, pushing herself up from the table and wrapping an arm around Kim's waist, the awful feeling spurring her into a selfish act of kindness. Although she's not quite as steady on her feet as she'd like to be, she's able to help support Kim's weight as she stumbles into the other room.

"Th-ah-n-kss," Kim mumbles.

Kim's head lolls onto her chest and her feet drag on the ground as Charlotte practically carries her. Once she gets close enough to the sofa, Charlotte lets go of Kim, who falls onto the cushions in a heap of gangly limbs, unconscious. Charlotte rolls Kim onto her back and heaves her legs onto the sofa for her, before sliding a small throw pillow underneath her head. Kim's mouth hangs open, a trail of drool leaking from the corner.

Charlotte can't help but feel another pang of regret at how she's been treating Kim. Although her jealousy is threatening to eat her alive and is making Kim's every action unbearable to her tonight, she knows that Kim has only ever genuinely loved her. She's always been there to provide feedback on every first draft, has attended every event, and has celebrated every one of her best friend's milestones.

Charlotte can't say the same about herself.

She brushes a strand of hair off of Kim's forehead, staring down at her face, before she turns to leave the room.

That's when she hears it.

The heaving. The gurgling. The coughs.

Charlotte turns around.

Kim lies with her eyes closed on the sofa, only now her body heaves and struggles as she chokes on her own vomit. The contents of her stomach spill over her chin and spray onto her shirt as her body struggles to breathe. Kim should be getting up, should be rolling onto her side, should be doing something, *anything,* to stop herself from choking, but she's out cold and unresponsive.

Charlotte reaches for Kim, ready to turn the woman onto her side, ready to help clear her airway, ready to call 9-1-1, ready to—

I was really hoping we'd have books out at the same time again.

Charlotte freezes in her tracks, her hand inches away from Kim.

She knows she should help her, but she doesn't.

Instead, Charlotte watches as Kim chokes and gags and heaves and sputters and, eventually, stops.

The house is silent.

In a haze, Charlotte stumbles to the entranceway and locks the front door before dragging herself upstairs. She crawls into bed fully dressed, lies on her side, and falls into an uneasy sleep.

It's not the light streaming through the open curtains that wakes Charlotte up but her pounding migraine. Pain shoots through her skull, lacing itself behind her eyeballs and burrowing deep into her temple. She checks the time on the alarm clock and exhales loudly; she has to wait another hour before she can take more acetaminophen. She grumbles to herself and rolls onto her stomach, burying her face in her pillow. She wants nothing more than to fall back asleep and forget about the drinking from the night before. Her tongue feels like cotton and the inside of her mouth tastes like the floor of a bar thanks to all the drinks she and Kim had last nig—

Kim.

Her chest tightens and she struggles for air as she slowly remembers her friend downstairs on the living room sofa. She pushes herself up in the bed, suddenly awake, and shakes her head.

No, there's no way, she tells herself, getting to her feet. She takes uneven steps across the bedroom floor, her body heavy from the alcohol and still slightly uncoordinated. She passes through the upstairs hallway and stops at the top of the staircase, holding onto the bannister with white knuckles.

"Kim?" she calls down. "Kim, are you up yet?"

The living room is silent.

"Kim?" she asks, louder.

No answer.

She slowly descends the steps, using the extra time to convince herself that she's misremembering the night before as the downstairs comes into view.

She went home.
But she was drunk.
She took an Uber home.
Her purse is still hanging up in the entrance.
She's forgetful.
Her boots are there, too.
She's very forgetful.

Charlotte knows what she'll find waiting for her in the living room, so she goes into the kitchen instead and opens the blinds, the light making her migraine worse as she avoids looking at Kim's car in the driveway, buried under a thick layer of snow. She opens the pantry and takes out a bag of coffee, scoops some into her drip machine's reusable filter, and closes the lid before starting the appliance. She listens as the coffee percolates, enjoying the sizzle as condensation builds up and water drips onto the burner of the ancient machine. The smell of the dark roast is almost enough to cover up the smell of the spilt liquor and stale vomit.

With a slow exhale, Charlotte peers into the living room from the kitchen doorway.

Kim lies on her back in the middle of the sofa, her right arm spilling off the edge. Her mouth hangs open and streaks of liquid run down her skin, trailing onto the cushions underneath her head. Unlike last night, her eyes are now open and lifeless as they stare up at the white ceiling.

Charlotte stares at Kim for a long time before rushing to the bathroom, lifting the lid of the toilet in the nick of time, and throwing up. She heaves, the contents of her stomach from the night before splashing against the side of the white porcelain bowl and into the crystal-clear water. It burns the back of her throat as the alcohol and bile force their way out of her system. When she's finally done, she flushes twice before rising to brush her teeth and splash water on her face.

Trying not to look at Kim again, Charlotte goes back into the kitchen and grabs her phone off of the counter she had left it on last night. She unlocks the screen, glad to see there's still some battery left, and dials 9-1-1.

"9-1-1, what's your emergency?" the agent says on the other end.

Charlotte opens her mouth to answer but freezes, not sure what to tell them.

I killed my friend?
I let her drown?
I wanted her to die?

"Hello?" the operator asks.

"My friend," Charlotte finally manages. "I found my friend dead on my couch."

It takes the ambulance twenty minutes to arrive at Charlotte's house while she waits on the phone with 9-1-1. She told them that her friend didn't have a pulse, wasn't breathing, and wasn't responsive, but they sent an ambulance anyway.

When the medics arrive to examine the body, they ask Charlotte the same questions the dispatcher had asked on the phone.

"How long ago did you find her?" one of them asks.

"About ten minutes ago. I came downstairs to put on coffee and I thought she was still sleeping. When I went to wake her up, I realized something was wrong."

"Where is she now?"

"Still on the sofa," Charlotte tells them, directing the pair to the living room, their boots trailing wet snow across the floor.

"Have you moved her?"

"No, I haven't touched her."

"Do you know if she's taken any medications or illicit substances?" they ask her, transferring Kim from her spot on the couch to the wood floor.

"Alcohol."

"When?"

"We were celebrating for most of last night."

"Do you know how much she had to drink?"

"I don't know. A lot. We both had a lot. I wasn't feeling good, so I went upstairs to bed and left her alone. She was finishing a glass of wine on the couch when I last saw her," she lies.

The paramedics try to revive Kim but ultimately pronounce her dead. They tell Charlotte to leave the body alone until the coroner's office can come and collect it, then they give her their condolences and leave.

Charlotte pours herself a coffee and drinks it in the kitchen, focusing her attention on the sun outside the window. She doesn't want to think about Kim or her cold body lying in the middle of the room only a few short metres from her.

It's another two hours before the coroner's office arrives, their squeaky van parking at the top of her driveway. Two older men carry their gurney and a bag up the front steps of the house, and Charlotte leads them through to the living room. After examining the area and collecting Kim's body, they tell her that an autopsy will confirm Kim's cause of death but they suspect it to be aspiration pneumonia. They add that Charlotte is free to use her living room again and is allowed to clean or dispose of her sofa, as a police investigation into Kim's death is not necessary at this time. Like the paramedics, they offer Charlotte their condolences, before hauling Kim's body down the front steps. She watches from the kitchen window as they load the metal gurney weighed down with her friend into the back of the van and drive away from her home, the wheels of the vehicle spinning hard on the ice.

As she sits in the empty kitchen, the weight of everything finally hits her, and she cries into her hands. When she's done, she gets up and opens the fridge, pulling out the white pastry box Kim had brought her and taking out a cupcake with bright blue frosting and edible pearls. She hums to herself, as she peels off the paper liner, the corner of her mouth lifting in a wry grin.

I guess our books aren't coming out at the same time after all.

February

"I'm so sorry for your loss," Emily says, leaning forward across the small table and taking Charlotte's hands in her own. "I know how close you and Kim were. I can't imagine any of this has been easy on you. Especially with the, well, you know," she says, gesturing to the room around them.

Charlotte nods tersely. She does know.

When her agent had called to meet with her off the clock for the first time since Kim's passing, Charlotte had been quick to suggest the bookstore by her house. Although it's just another Azure Pages, the largest book retailer in Canada with identical stores everywhere, the one near her house is outfitted with a coffee shop on the second floor. The drinks are never good and they cost her three times as much as it would to make them at home, but she's always loved coming here for the ambiance.

Unfortunately, Charlotte hadn't gotten the memo that all Azure Pages locations across the country were paying tribute to Kim's national legacy by plastering her name and face all over the store, along with endcap displays of her books. No matter where Charlotte goes in the store, it feels like Kim's eyes are on her.

She pulls her hands out of Emily's, who gives her a sad smile while she takes a sip of her coffee from the white disposable cup.

Those are so bad for the environment, Kim used to tell her, always making a point to bring her reusable mug wherever she went. *It's because of the plastic coating they use on the inside of the cups. You can't separate it from the paper, so it makes the cups impossible to recycle. You should—*

"Yeah, I just can't believe she's gone," Charlotte says, drumming her fingers on the table.

"And it's been three weeks since she passed?"

"A month," she says, discreetly checking her phone for the time.

"Wow, already?"

"Yeah, but it feels like it was only yesterday. The pain is so fresh, you know?"

As much as Charlotte hates to admit it, it *has* been a difficult couple of weeks for her. Since Kim's death, her house hasn't felt the same. There's a weight to the air inside the living room that wasn't there before her friend died, and the couch... she can't even look at the couch anymore.

To make matters worse, her phone has been blowing up with calls and messages from people looking to get more information about the circumstances of Kim's sudden death; everyone from reporters to friends to complete strangers has reached out to her. Although she was reluctant to say anything at first, worried that someone would somehow figure out what she'd really done—or, perhaps more accurately, hadn't done—to Kim, she soon realized that this was an opportunity she couldn't pass up to get her name out. While she's never so gauche as to promote her new novel outright, she doesn't hold back the details of its release whenever she's asked how she knew Kim.

"I can't even imagine what you must be feeling right now," Emily says now, eyes welling up out of sympathy for Charlotte. "I know we've mostly had a working relationship, but I mean it when I say I'm here for you if you need anything."

"Thanks, Em, I really, *really* appreciate it, but I think, right now, the best thing for me is to try and focus on other things, you know?"

"Oh, of course. But when you're ready, I'm here for you."

"Thanks," Charlotte says with a small, grateful smile.

Emily nods and leans back in her chair as Charlotte takes another deep sip of her drink. It's clear that the other woman wants to ask her something, but Charlotte is eager to leave the store and the watchful eyes of the cardboard Kims. She checks the time again as Emily bends down, searching for something in her large purse which rests on the floor next to her chair. She takes out a galley—the white sheets of a manuscript bound together but still coverless—and puts it face down on the table.

"Look, I told the publisher I didn't feel right asking you about this, but they were insistent," she says, shifting uncomfortably in her seat and avoiding Charlotte's gaze. She pushes the galley towards Charlotte but leaves her hand on the back of it when Charlotte reaches for it. "You're allowed to say no, okay?"

Charlotte picks the book up and flips it over, revealing the title page with a note written in pen.

OF CHAMPAGNE PROMISES
by Kim Lavoie

MAGNUM OPUS

Note: Please keep the foreword to <500 words due to space constraints. Please return by March 1st for production deadline. Release date: Aprill 11th.

She stares at the ink on the clean white paper, her mouth bone dry and her chest tight. It feels like she's breathing air through a straw and her hands shake as she grabs the table to keep herself from falling over in her seat. She looks up from the page, eyes flickering around the interior of the book shop like she's searching for help. All she finds are the disapproving smiles of Kim, who watches her from the posters all around the store.

Charlotte tries to find the right wording but eventually settles on a simple, "What the fuck is this?"

"It's Kim's new book."

"I pieced that much together," Charlotte hisses. "But what do they want from me?"

"They want you to write the foreword for it, since you were Kim's best friend. She always talked about how close you both were, so naturally, you were the obvious choice for this."

"But her book isn't coming out. She's dead. They wouldn't put out her book this soon after she—"

"I thought it was in bad taste too, but the publisher wanted to move forward with it and her family has given them their blessing, so it's still coming out in April. Which is great because it means you'll get to share a new-release shelf with her one last time."

I was really hoping we'd have books out at the same time again.

Charlotte stares down at the manuscript, her face flushed and her lips dry.

"But if you're not up to it, I understand," Emily adds.

Charlotte looks up from the white pages and stops, her body freezing and heart skipping a beat.

Kim stares back at her from right behind Emily.

"What the fuck?" Charlotte shouts, standing up from her seat so quickly that her chair tips over and crashes onto the ground behind her, drawing her gaze. When she looks back up, Kim is gone.

Emily clutches her chest and leans away from Charlotte in her seat.

"I'm sorry! I just... They asked and I thought you might be okay with it! I'll tell them no!"

Charlotte cranes her neck, trying to spot her dead friend in the sea of patrons. People are watching her with confusion, her sudden outburst having attracted the attention of both customers and staff. They eye her with worry, uncertain if she's about to have another outburst. When she doesn't see the Kim lookalike again in the crowd, she leans over the second storey bannister to stare at the customers in the bookstore below. If any of them heard her yell, they're not paying attention now as they browse the rows of books, reading back covers and putting novels away on the wrong shelves. The only Kims she sees now are on the posters, watching her with their manufactured smiles.

Charlotte exhales through pursed lips before she picks up her chair, drags it back to her spot at the table, and takes a seat across from her agent.

"Are... are you okay?" Emily asks, clutching the gold chain she wears around her neck.

"Sorry, I just..." She trails off, not sure how to finish her sentence. *Saw Kim? Saw something? Lost my mind?* She shakes her head apologetically, gesturing around the Azure Pages and at the manuscript. "I got really overwhelmed. It's been a lot, you know?"

Emily nods, on edge but warming back up to Charlotte. "I can't even imagine."

"I'm sorry I freaked out. That wasn't okay of me."

"No, you don't need to apologise for anything! I shouldn't have told them I'd ask you about the—"

"I'll do it. I'll write the foreword."

"Really? Are you sure?"

"Of course. There's nothing else I'd rather do to honour Kim's memory," she lies.

Charlotte closes the car door and locks it with the key fob before resting her head on her steering wheel, exhausted. Emily left almost fifteen minutes earlier, and Charlotte is thankful for the alone time without having to worry about whether her agent will stumble upon her like this in the driver's seat of her car. Especially when she's likely still freaked out by Charlotte's outburst in the coffee shop.

I was really hoping we'd have books out at the same time again.

"Fuck! Fuck! Fuuuuuck!" Charlotte screams at the top of her lungs, face buried in the leather steering wheel. She's furious with Kim, Kim's publisher, and—although she doesn't want to admit it—herself.

She can feel the question rooting around the back of her brain, weaseling its way into her train of thought.

Did I let Kim die for nothing?

She shoves her keys into the ignition, the engine roaring to life, and puts the car from 'park' to 'drive.' As she's pulling out of the Azure Pages parking lot, she swears she can still see one of Kim's posters watching her from inside the store.

She hangs her keys on the hook by the door and kicks her boots off onto the plastic mat in the entranceway, reminding herself all the while that spring is nearly here, before unzipping her coat and hanging it in the small closet. She fishes Kim's galley out of her purse. The manuscript feels heavy in her hands despite its meagre size, and Charlotte wants nothing more than to throw it into her recycling bin and forget that she ever met with Emily at the Azure Pages.

Unfortunately, she knows that's not an option, and she brings the book into the kitchen with her and sets it down on the butcher's block.

OF CHAMPAGNE PROMISES
by Kim Lavoie

She rolls her eyes at the title. She's always thought Kim picked gaudy names for her books that would keep readers away, not that anyone—or even Kim's sales—agrees with her on the matter.

It's always frustrated Charlotte how successful Kim has been with her writing in comparison to herself. She's always thought that her own work is more meaningfully created, insightful into the human condition, while Kim's is, at times, tawdry and pedestrian. It bothers her that the masses don't agree.

Charlotte flips the book open, eyes glazing over as she scans the publisher information and legal jargon. She turns to the next page and stops at the dedication.

Charlotte,
I wouldn't be where I am today if it weren't for you.
Your friend, forever,
Kim.

She exhales slowly, gripping the counter as she steadies herself, her eyes watering. The emotions hit her like they have these past four weeks: in waves of grief and regret that come unexpectedly and grab at her, threatening to pull her under, before letting her go just as quickly. As much as she's had moments throughout their long friendship where she disliked Kim—even wondering if she hated her at times—she still loved her, in her own confusing and conflicted way, and looked to her as a source of comfort. Although Charlotte had been guiltily glad to be rid of her in the moment, thinking Kim's absence could make room for her to finally get the recognition she deserves, she hadn't anticipated just how much she'd miss her friend.

She closes the book and wipes her tears with the back of her hand as the familiar sadness slowly releases its hold on her. She doesn't want to waste her evening crying over Kim, but she doesn't know if she'll be able to get through the book while sober. Charlotte opens the small cabinet above her kitchen sink, the hinges squeaking despite being fairly new. She takes out a wine glass, carelessly smudging fingerprints onto the crystal-clear bowl, before pulling open one of the stainless-steel doors of the fridge. She grabs a half-full bottle of white wine and pours herself a generous amount, enjoying the sweet floral bouquet, before returning the bottle to its shelf.

She leans against the island and takes a swig from her glass. She swallows fast, lips puckering from the harsh flavour that coats the inside of her mouth and drips down her throat.

"Ugh!"

The alcohol is bitter and overly acidic, like it's gone sour. She swirls the wine around in the glass, smelling it, nostrils flaring at its pungent scent. It didn't stink when she opened the bottle, but now it fills the air with a rancid odour. She makes a face and dumps the remainder of her glass down the kitchen sink before getting the bottle back out of the fridge to pour out the last of it.

The smell fills the kitchen and makes the air feel thick. Her head swims. She waves a hand in front of her nose, trying to disperse the smell, but it only makes her feel dizzier. She leans against the counter, noticing Kim's book out of the corner of her eye, and grabs the galley before escaping the stink of the kitchen for the fresh air of the living room.

She tries not to stare at the couch that Kim died on, but she can't help herself.

Charlotte avoided the living room for the first week after her friend's death. There was something about the room that made her uncomfortable, made her feel *guilty*, and so she started spending more time in her kitchen and up in her bedroom than she ever had before. Of course, having watched Kim die, it made sense to her at first that she'd have trouble being around where it happened. But then the feeling only got stronger, so much so that Charlotte couldn't help but be overcome with dread every time she set foot in the living room. Not wanting to annex off a part of her house, she decided it wasn't the living room that was the problem but the couch itself. Although she'd had the fabric professionally cleaned, something about the sofa and its worn down cushions left her unsettled, so she bought a cover for them hoping it would help.

It didn't.

While the couch certainly looked different—the vintage plum cushions now covered with flamingo pink and decorated with throw pillows in gaudy floral covers reading things like "Home Is Where the Books Are!" and "Plans Were Meant to Be Cancelled!"—it still made Charlotte uncomfortable. The cushions where Kim had fallen asleep looked perpetually weighed down. No matter how much she fluffed them, no matter how much she rearranged the couch covers, and no matter how many blankets she piled under the cushions to lift them higher, they constantly looked flat.

Like Kim was still lying down on them.

A chill passes down Charlotte's spine and she looks away from the couch, moving through the room to her comfortable leather recliner stationed across from the sofa. She stumbles, her feet heavy as she moves, and she realises that it's not the smell from the kitchen that's gotten to her but the wine itself.

She's drunk.

Her head feels fuzzy, her thoughts like the white noise and crackling static of a dead TV channel, and her every step is clumsy and fumbling. Her mouth is dry like sand and her face is hot to the touch. She falls onto her chair, dropping the galley onto the ground beside her. Her head lolls forward and she feels nauseous. With how uncoordinated she's become, she can't help but worry that she won't make it to the bathroom in time if she needs to hurl.

She blinks, confused as to how one sip of spoiled wine could send her over the edge, and she sees her.

Kim.

Lying on the couch.

Charlotte's heart beats so fast that she's sure it's going to give out at any second. She stares at her dead friend who looks up at the ceiling, unmoving, with a blank expression on her face, her mouth hanging open like it did the night she died. Her chest is still and she doesn't blink, but there's something about her that makes Charlotte feel like she could jump up at any second.

"K-Kim," she finally breathes.

Her friend is silent.

"Kim? I-sthatyo-ou?" she slurs.

Kim remains quiet, body still, and Charlotte opens her mouth to say something else but stops, sucking her breath in as Kim turns her head towards her. The other woman's eyes are hollow, empty, and they don't look *at* her, they look *through* her. Charlotte feels sick as Kim lies silently on the cushions with her gaze fixed on Charlotte's face. She can't look away as liquid begins to leak out of Kim's open mouth, colourless droplets spilling over her lips and running down her chin and over her cheeks, dribbling onto the light couch covers and leaving wet trails down the side of the sofa.

Charlotte sits up in her recliner with a start, her cellphone's ringer blaring in the entranceway. She stares at the sofa, her muscles tensing and pulse throbbing under her skin as she prepares herself to see Kim lying on the wet cushions, watching her.

But the couch is empty.

Her phone goes momentarily silent in the other room before ringing again, her cute ringer sounding obnoxious in the silence of her home. She gets up from her chair with a groan, her head pounding and stomach churning, and drags herself up to the entrance. She reaches into her purse, searching through her belongings for her phone, before pulling it out on the last ring.

"What?" she asks, not in the mood for pleasantries.

"Where are you?" Emily shouts, making Charlotte wince.

"I'm at home, why? What's wrong?"

"I've been calling you for like an hour! You were supposed to do that interview with—"

"Oh, shit!" Charlotte groans, slapping a palm to her forehead in frustration. The sudden jolt seems to jar her sore head and she squeezes her eyes shut in pain. "I completely forgot!"

"Yeah. They weren't exactly thrilled about being stood up."

"I'm sorry, I didn't mean to. I just, I don't know, I overslept."

"I figured as much. Thankfully, I was able to reschedule it with them."

"To when?"

"Check your email. I sent you a calendar invite."

"Thanks," Charlotte says, relieved.

"Try not to miss that one too, okay?"

"Sorry, Emily. Really, I am."

Her agent sighs on the other end of the line. "It's fine. I told them you've been having a hard time lately and needed the day off because of everything with Kim."

Charlotte can't help but laugh. "You're not wrong there."

"You know," Emily says, hesitantly, "you *really* don't have to write that foreword if it's too difficult right now. I know Kim's death hasn't been easy for you and—"

"It's fine. Really."

"I just mean that—"

"I need to go. Sorry, I'll talk to you soon. Thanks for rescheduling the interview."

She hangs up before Emily can say goodbye.

The hair on the back of her neck bristles and the air behind her feels heavy. She spins around, half-expecting Kim to be back in the living room, lying on the couch, judging her with dead eyes.

But no one's there.

She exhales loudly and rubs at her chest with one hand, feeling her heart beating fast beneath her breastbone. She lifts her phone again and types a few keywords into her browser, hitting search. She dials the first number that shows up on the screen.

"Hey there! I was just looking to book a mover. I have a couch that I need to get rid of."

Charlotte thanks the barista, slipping a fiver into the tip cup before heading to her favourite seat in the Azure Pages coffee shop. It's a small table hidden away from the perpetually long line of patrons and out of reach from the handful of power outlets people always seem to need to use. It's also, crucially, next to the shop's second-story bannister, allowing her to sip her coffee upstairs while looking out into the stacks of books below. Although it is one of the noisier seats in the cafe, allowing both the sounds from the Azure Pages and the coffee shop to crash over her, it's still her favourite spot to relax.

She places *Of Champagne Promises* on the round table and sips her expensive drink. As much as she hates carrying Kim's galley around in public, she hates the idea of reading it at home even more. The feeling in her house has only gotten worse since her dream about Kim on her sofa a few nights ago. Although she knows it's all in her head, likely a result of the stressful day she'd had with Emily, she can't shake the feeling that she's never alone in her house anymore.

The thought chills her and so she takes an even bigger sip of her drink to try and warm her bones back up.

OF CHAMPAGNE PROMISES
by Kim Lavoie

Charlotte opens the galley, making sure to skip past the dedication and the customary note from the publisher explaining that the book has been published posthumously at the request of Kim's family and with the blessings of her friends. *Which* friends gave the book their blessing, Charlotte will never know. She certainly didn't. Although she's agreed to write the foreword for the book, shamefully hoping that displaying her name in Kim's final novel might help her own sales, she has no intention of actually reading the manuscript.

As she flips through the pages, a sentence a few chapters in catches her eye. She takes a large sip as she reads:

"'You must be excited,' Riley says, taking a seat at the mahogany table as Willow puts out a set of old champagne flutes that were gifted to her at her wedding.

'I am! But it's really not that big of a deal. I kind of feel silly celebrating, to be honest,' she says, blushing scarlet.

'Why would you be embarrassed?'

'I don't know. I just, I guess it's not that big of a deal,' she says, trying to downplay the importance of her situation."

Charlotte stares at the page, struggling to swallow as the hot drink burns her mouth. She reads ahead, not wanting to continue but unable to stop herself.

"'It's a huge deal,' the woman argues. 'You have a book coming out! What's not to get excited about?'

'I don't know. I mean, it's not like it's my first one. And there are bigger names in the business...'

'So?' Riley cries. 'Don't sell yourself short! Oh, this is going to be so great! I was really hoping we'd have books out at the same time again!'

'Wait... are you saying that—'

'Yes! I wanted to wait to tell you in person because it's so exciting, but we have books coming out at the same time!'

'I'm so happy for you!' Willow shouts, disingenuous.

'Come on!' Riley lifts her champagne glass high in the air. 'To our success!'"

Charlotte feels like the walls of the Azure Pages are closing in on her, slowly encroaching on her peace of mind and personal safety. She looks up from the galley and around the store, eyes immediately zeroing in on one of the large posters of Kim hanging from the ceiling.

It looks... wrong.

Kim's picture-perfect smile is gone, replaced by a blank expression and dull eyes. She stares down at Charlotte from her poster's spot high in the air. Charlotte looks away but finds herself locking eyes with another poster of Kim, this one looking up at her from its position on an endcap in the store below. Her pulse quickens as she looks around the room, spotting yet another poster of Kim near the entrance of the cafe. This one looks to the left, eyes seeing her through the doorway. She whips her head around, finding each poster of Kim and realizing the same thing over and over again: it's not a trick of the light, each photo *is* looking straight at her.

A hundred Kims, all watching her.

She slams the book closed, gets up from her spot at the table, and hurries to the escalator, breathing hard and fast.

All of the faces turn and move, their dead eyes following Charlotte as she leaves.

"I'm not trying to harangue you, Charlotte," Emily chastises over the phone, "but the deadline is in a couple of days and I haven't even gotten a draft from you."

"I know, I *know*. I'm working on it. You'll get it tomorrow."

"Will I? Actually? Because you've told me this twice now, and each time I check my inbox, I don't find anything from you."

"I mean it," Charlotte says, running a hand through her hair as she leans back in the bed, trying to get comfortable against the stack of pillows propped up between herself and the wooden headboard.

"Good, because I'm counting on you. You had me tell the publisher that you were going to write this foreword, despite my better judgement, and now they're pestering me to pester you."

"I know, I *knooooow*," she moans. Her laptop sits open on the comforter beside her, the black cursor blinking on the empty white page. "I'm almost done," she tells her agent, wondering how to even start.

"Tomorrow, Charlotte. I want to see it in my inbox. Got it?"

"Sir, yes sir," Charlotte jokes, saluting to herself.

"If it's not in by tomorrow morning, I'm telling them you're not going to write it."

"Fine," she grumbles. "Have a good night, Em."

"And you have a productive one," Emily says, the line going dead.

Charlotte clicks the power button on the side of the phone, her screen fading to black. She catches her reflection in the blackened glass, trying not to notice the bags under her eyes, her wiry hair, or Kim's eyes staring back at her from the screen.

She throws the phone onto the bed and slides the computer back onto her lap, pressing the backlight button a few times to make sure the screen is bright enough that it's blinding. She focuses on the cursor, avoiding the empty space on the monitor where she knows Kim's eyes now live.

Her friend's hollow stare followed her home from the store over a week ago and has infected her life ever since. Old photos of Charlotte and Kim no longer look like happy memories but are instead reminders of what she'd allowed to happen, reminders of what she'd done. Then she started seeing Kim's eyes in the empty spaces between, like when she's looking in the mirror or into the reflection of the TV or even at night in the blackness of her home. It's always the same: just two expressionless eyes watching her from somewhere that isn't *here*.

She clicks away at the keyboard, trying not to notice the eyes in the top right of her screen as she works, hoping they'll go away but knowing they won't. As she hammers out a poor excuse for a foreword, her computer flashes a warning: BATTERY AT 5%.

She reaches for the power cord, sliding her hand across the comforter as she searches for it before she remembers that she left it downstairs on the kitchen island. She exhales loudly. She doesn't want to have to go downstairs. Not with Kim just—

She tries not to finish the sentence in her mind, worried that she might give the idea power by even imagining her dead friend just—

She shakes her head, stopping herself again. She gets up from the bed and steps quickly through the second-floor hallway and down the stairs. She tries to avoid looking into the living room, afraid of what she'll see there, but she can't help herself as curiosity gets the best of her.

Her new sofa sits where the old one used to, with a modern design and crisp marigold yellow fabric that pays homage to sofas of the seventies. It's not quite what she wanted, but she was desperate to get something, *anything*, to replace the sofa that Kim had died on, with its cheap cover and sunken cushions.

When the movers had come for the old couch, it had felt like a weight had been lifted from her life. Although she'd only seen Kim in her living room that one time, she'd avoided being around the sullied furniture since the apparition. It had taken nearly a week for the store to deliver her new sofa, and while the air in the house hadn't felt any lighter—even though Charlotte tried pretending like it had—she'd felt a bit safer.

But after the new couch had been delivered, she'd realized how wrong she'd been. Even before the movers had left, the cushions had started to look weighed down and sunken in, like someone was laying on them. She'd tried refusing the delivery but had already signed the papers. When she'd called the store with her complaints, they'd sent another team to collect the sofa and replace it with one that wasn't defective. But when the team came, no one but Charlotte could see the indents in the cushions. They still replaced the new couch with an even newer one, but the cushions were flat again when they left.

They're still flat now as Charlotte looks into the living room from the doorway of the kitchen. Although the couch unsettles her on its own, it's worse when Kim is there, lying on the sofa with her dead eyes looking up, always staring, like she can see through the floor and into Charlotte's bedroom. After the initial apparition that she'd written off as a dream, she didn't see Kim again for almost two weeks. When she did, it was while she was in the kitchen making toast. She felt something in the other room, like the air was heavy once more, and when she peered into the living room, Kim was back on the sofa staring into nothingness.

And then, in another blink, Kim was gone.

It happened again the day after, when Charlotte was in the entranceway pulling on her boots to go for a walk. The couch was empty and then, suddenly, it wasn't. She'd gone for her walk, hoping the crisp air would clear her head, but when she returned home, Kim was exactly where she'd left her. She stayed there for the better part of the day before vanishing into thin air and leaving Charlotte alone once again. Each time she appeared it was the same: she lay on her back in the middle of the couch, her arm spilling off the sofa and hanging onto the ground, dead eyes looking up at the ceiling. Each time she appeared, to Charlotte's frustration and mounting dread, she stayed a little longer.

Thankfully, the room is empty tonight and Charlotte breathes a sigh of relief as she grabs her power cord off the kitchen island. She turns around but then pauses, deciding to take advantage of the empty first floor while she has the chance. She quickly brews herself a tea and assembles a peanut butter and jelly sandwich before heading back upstairs.

As she leaves the kitchen, she sees Kim.

Although she's still in the living room, she's no longer on the couch.

Instead, she stands at the head of the sofa where Charlotte stood the night Kim died, and stares at her friend with her dead eyes and her vacant expression.

Charlotte runs up the stairs, spilling the hot tea over the edge of the mug and onto her hand as she moves. Even after she slams the door behind her, she can feel Kim watching her from the living room below.

March

Charlotte takes the keys out of her purse and slides them into the lock but doesn't turn them.

Not yet.

She leans her head against the cold wood of her front door and steadies herself, mentally preparing for whatever is waiting for her inside. Except she knows what's waiting in her house. It's the same thing that's been tormenting her for over a month now: Kim.

She sighs and turns the keys, the tumblers clicking into place as the door unlatches and swings slowly open. Her house is dark, the only light coming from the microwave that hangs over the range. The radio plays softly on the counter, some glam rock song from the eighties that she recognizes but can't sing along with, and she closes the door behind her. She hangs her jacket up along with her purse, kicks her shoes off onto the mat, and keeps her eyes glued to the floor—trying to ignore Kim's reflection in the hardwood—as she moves from the entrance into the kitchen.

She flips the switch on the wall, the room quickly filling with light, and she picks up the silver kettle off of the stove, ignoring

Kim's reflection in the dull metal, before filling it with water. She sets it down on the burner before grabbing a mug, throwing in an Earl Grey tea bag, and adding two spoons of sugar into the empty ceramic cup. She leans against the counter, staring down at her feet, while the water boils. She doesn't need to see Kim's dead eyes in the kitchen tile to know she's being watched by the other woman.

Kim's movements around the house have been getting progressively worse. At first, she'd just lain on the couch, looking up at the ceiling. Then she'd started standing at the head of the sofa, watching Charlotte's every move. Then she'd started roaming the ground floor. Charlotte had discovered this while washing her hands in the bathroom, trying not to notice Kim's eyes in the hollows of the mirror. She'd opened the door to find Kim waiting on the other side of it. She'd screamed and locked herself in the washroom for almost thirty minutes, hyperventilating, before she'd finally found the courage to leave the room. The next time it had happened, Charlotte had been in bed sleeping when she'd felt Kim's presence in the room with her. When she'd opened her eyes, Kim had been standing at the foot of her bed, watching from the blackness. Charlotte hadn't gotten much sleep that night, or any of the ones that followed, for that matter.

Much like she's grown to accept Kim's eyes in the empty spaces of her life, or her dead body on the sunken living room cushions, she's eventually grown to accept that Kim will appear—and disappear—around the house at random. But just because she's come to accept the fact of it doesn't mean she can stand the feeling of those empty eyes staring back at her, and so she avoids looking anywhere she doesn't have to.

The kettle hisses and howls, filling the small space with noise. Charlotte turns the burner off, picks the kettle up by its heat-resistant handle, and pours the scalding liquid into her cup. She takes a metal spoon and stirs everything together in her glass before putting the utensil on the counter and leaving her tea to steep.

Her phone buzzes in her pocket and she fishes it out, making sure the screen is illuminated—the bright light helps drown out Kim's stares—before she looks at it. It's an advertisement forwarded by her agent. She scans the email.

I wasn't sure if you were on the mailing list for these notifications, but I thought I'd pass them along in case you wanted to see them. If you don't, or if it's too much, just tell me. I'll make sure they don't come your way.

— Emily

Charlotte scrolls down to the forwarded email, reading the header to herself.

An Excerpt from The Surefire Hit
OF CHAMPAGNE PROMISES
Kim Lavoie's Final Novel
Available Everywhere April 11

The words strike a chord and she can't stop her eyes from watering as she rereads her friend's byline. It's Kim's last book, but in her heart she knows it didn't have to be. She just wanted her chance to make it big, to have her moment, to be recognized for her *art*, but even in death Kim overshadows her. The more she thinks about the night Kim died, the more she's filled with regret.

She keeps reading.

"She laughs, letting go of the wooden chair and trying her luck standing on her own. Her legs shake and her body wobbles with each small step she takes as she tries to get to the leather sofa, her eyes struggling to stay open. Charlotte—"

She rubs her eyes, sure she's reading the excerpt wrong, but the name is still there when she reads it a second time. Kim's eyes watch from the corner of her screen as she continues.

"Charlotte is tempted to stick a leg out as Kim passes her by—"

Charlotte thinks she's about to throw up.

"—but stops herself when she imagines all the possible things the woman could crash into and break if she were to fall."

She skips ahead, stomach uneasy as she reads.

"Kim's head lolls onto her chest and she struggles to walk, her feet dragging on the ground as Charlotte practically carries her. Once she gets close enough to the sofa, Charlotte lets go of Kim, who falls onto it in a heap of clumsy limbs and dead weight. She rolls Kim onto her back and arranges her on the couch, struggling to lift her legs onto the cushions and slide a small throw pillow

underneath her head. Kim's mouth hangs open, a trail of drool leaking from the corner of the unconscious woman's mouth."

She shakes her head, unable to believe the words printed on the page.

*"She brushes a strand of hair off of Kim's forehead, staring down at her face, before she turns to leave the room.
That's when she hears it.
The heaving. The gurgling. The coughs.
Charlotte turns around.
Kim lies with her eyes closed on the sofa, only now her body heaves and struggles as she chokes on her own vomit."*

Charlotte holds onto the counter for support, suddenly lightheaded as she reads her own transgressions from that night, almost two full months ago, spelled out in the email.

*"Charlotte freezes in her tracks, her hand inches away from Kim. She knows she should help her, knows she should turn her onto her side, knows she should do something.
But she doesn't.
Instead, Charlotte watches as Kim chokes and gags and heaves and sputters and, eventually, stops.
The house is silent."*

Charlotte drops her phone onto the ground, her hands sweaty and shaking as she tries to make sense of what she's read.

She picks up the phone, face flushed and mouth dry, and skims over the email once more.

An Excerpt from The Surefire Hit
OF CHAMPAGNE PROMISES
Kim Lavoie's Final Novel
Available Everywhere April 11

"'No!' Riley screams, thrashing violently on the chaise longue. But it's no use.

Strong hands hold her down in the dark and force her mouth open, chipping one of her teeth as the heavy glass bottle is forced into her mouth. The assailant covers her nose and forces her head back, the liquor burning its way down her throat as she coughs and chokes on it. She kicks out, trying to free herself as the bottle is removed from her lips but soon another one takes its place and more liquid is poured down her throat.

Riley coughs, choking on the alcohol and getting dizzy fast. Everyone knows she's a lightweight and gets easily drunk off a glass of wine. She doesn't want to think about what this will do to her.

She manages to land a kick in her attacker's gut, forcing them off of her and into the moonlight that streams through her curtains.

'You?' she asks, clutching her stomach and wobbling on her feet. It's the last thing she says before the world fades to black."

OF CHAMPAGNE PROMISES
The Final Novel of Kim Lavoie

Available For Pre-Order Online or Wherever Books Are Sold

Charlotte stares at her phone for a long time before clicking the power button on the side of the device, shutting the screen off, too startled from what she's read to care that Kim's eyes watch her through the black glass.

Exhaustion hits her body like a brick, her legs turning to jelly and her eyes heavy. A migraine she didn't know she had pulsates behind her eye, and she decides to abandon her tea on the counter and go to bed. She turns off the kitchen lights and makes her way to the staircase, using the flashlight on the back of her phone to guide her.

Kim watches from the ground floor as Charlotte begins to ascend the stairs, her hand gripping the bannister tightly. She can't help herself and looks over her shoulder at Kim.

"I was really hoping we'd have books out at the same time again," Kim says as she looks up at Charlotte with her dead eyes and vacant expression.

Charlotte turns back to the stairs and heads to bed.

Charlotte sits in the living room recliner, her computer resting on her lap, and her eyes closed. She thinks of the sentence she wants to write, rewording it in her brain over and over again until it's perfect, before opening her eyes and typing it fast on the keyboard. She tries not to look at the eyes that follow her in the white screen of the laptop, tries not to focus on Kim watching her from the couch, and tries to tune out the blaring noise as she writes. Once the sentence is down, she closes her eyes and tries to focus on wording the next one.

Kim was always talkative in life and, much to Charlotte's ire, she'd grown talkative in death too. But where her voice was once light and melodic, it's now breathy and metallic, like she's whispering into a tin can. Even more frustrating to her is that Kim only repeats the same sentence.

"I was really hoping we'd have books out at the same time again."

At first, she'd said the line sporadically once or twice a day; then, she started saying it every hour. Now, she whispers to Charlotte constantly, a hum that doesn't stop and fills every corner of the house.

Having decided that any noise is better than the incessant whispers of Kim, Charlotte has been blasting the radio in her kitchen and keeps the television on 24/7. But even with the obnoxious commercials, eighties rock, and excitable talk show hosts, she can still hear Kim, a faint white noise that undercuts all the other sounds. She's so distracted by Kim's voice at the moment that she almost doesn't hear the doorbell.

She closes the laptop and rises from the chair, dropping the computer onto the seat behind her, staring at the floor as she moves through the house to answer her door. She keeps her eyes downcast and brushes a hand through her hair, knowing she's a mess. She hasn't been able to look in a mirror for a while, not without seeing Kim staring back at her. She turns the lock and opens the door.

Emily stands on her front steps, arms crossed over her chest and annoyance written on her face.

"So, you're not dead."

"What?" Charlotte asks, upset by the question.

"Well, I just figured you must be dead because you haven't been answering your calls or emails for the last week," Emily says, pushing past Charlotte and into the house. "Buuuut I guess you've just been ignoring me."

"Wait," Charlotte says, not turning around. She doesn't want to look back at Kim, who she knows is waiting for her inside her home. She wants to go out and have this conversation with Emily anywhere else. "How about we grab a coffee? My treat. We can talk about everything th—"

"I don't want coffee, Charlotte. I just want to know what's going on with you. You haven't been yourself since Kim died and I'm really worried about you."

Reluctantly, Charlotte closes the front door and turns to face Emily but keeps her eyes on the ground.

"I'm sorry. Things have just been really... stressful lately. I guess."

"Because of Kim?"

"Yeah," she admits.

"Have you thought about looking at therapy? Or maybe a grief counsellor?"

Charlotte shakes her head.

"Maybe it's something you should consider doin—Christ, why is everything so loud in here?" Emily interrupts herself, annoyed. She moves into the kitchen and turns off the radio before heading into the living room.

"Oh, no, please," Charlotte starts as Emily picks up the remote. "I like the noise. It's helpful and—"

Emily shuts off the TV and Charlotte finally looks up at her, trying not to let her distress show on her face. Kim stands directly behind Emily, her hushed whispers filling the space between them.

"How do you do anything with that racket? I could hardly hear myself think."

"I just... I prefer it." She doesn't add that anything is better than the sound of Kim's whispers. She doesn't imagine that would go over well with her agent.

"Look," Emily continues, her tone softening. "I need to know you're taking things seriously when it comes to the release of your next book. I think it's your best one yet and I want it to be successful. Don't you?"

Charlotte nods in agreement, although she struggles to hear Emily's words. Kim's whispers are loud and distracting, and she can't help but look around the room as she tries to avoid Kim's vacant eyes that watch her from behind the other woman.

"Good. Then I need you to put in the work. You can't keep cancelling interviews or public readings or any of the shit you've been doing," Emily says, frustrated. "I'm doing everything I can to help move preorders and get people excited about your novel before it comes out, but I can only do so much. *You* have to do the rest."

Charlotte nods again, eyes glued to Kim as Emily talks.

"I really need you to work at this," Emily says, a raspiness entering her voice. "You were so excited about this book, and now... it's like the love has died."

Charlotte looks back at the ground, the weight of Kim's stare too much right now.

"I'm sorry. I didn't mean to, I just—"

"I was really hoping we'd have books out at the same time again," Emily says, voice rattling.

Charlotte's eyes snap up, her heart jumping into her throat.

Emily stares at Charlotte with hollow eyes and a vacant expression. Her mouth hangs open and liquid pools over her lips and drips down her chin.

"What did you say?" Charlotte asks, voice small.

"I was really hoping we'd have books out at the same time again," she repeats.

"Kim?" Charlotte asks Emily tentatively. "Is that you?"

"Why did you do it?" Kim asks through the other woman.

"What?"

"I thought we were friends."

"We-we were."

"Were we?" she asks, moving towards Charlotte. Charlotte takes a step back. "You let me die. You didn't care and you let me die."

"Kim, I never meant to—"

"How could you just let me die?"

She takes another step forward.

"I didn't mean to!" Charlotte cries, shoving Emily away from her.

Her agent falls backwards in the living room, crashing onto the floor hard. She looks up at Charlotte, her blank expression replaced by one of fear and confusion. Charlotte blinks down at her.

"Emily?"

"What the fuck is wrong with you?" Emily shouts defensively, pushing herself back up. Charlotte reaches out a shaking hand.

"I'm... so sorry. I thought—"

"Don't touch me!" Emily yells, yanking herself away from Charlotte and giving her a wide berth as she storms out of the room.

"Emily, I'm sorry! I don't know what happened. I just... Please, I'm sorry!"

Emily doesn't look back as she takes off out the front door.

Charlotte's phone vibrates on the coffee table as the email notification comes in. She looks down at the screen, unlocking the phone, and opens the email she's been expecting all week.

Emily has dropped her as a client.

Charlotte sits on the steps of her house, the clouds overhead threatening to bring rain. She doesn't care that it's cold or grey out. She's just relieved to be out of the house, even if she can still feel Kim's eyes on the back of her neck and hear the perpetual whispering.

She can hear it no matter where she goes.

She discovered this when she left her house to get groceries and Kim's whispers followed her all the way to the supermarket. She could see Kim's eyes in her back mirror and in the reflection of the store windows. She could see Kim in her backseat, in the parking lot, and at the end of every aisle.

It doesn't matter where she runs to, Kim follows.

But at least outside, she can find solace in the cold breeze and fresh air.

She watches her breath come out in white clouds, cutting through the air before fading to nothing. The day is still winter cold despite the lack of snow on the ground and she's excited for spring.

As she's lost in thought, a brown van pulls up and stops at the top of her driveway. A man gets out and opens the back, grabbing a small box out of the vehicle before approaching her.

"Char—"

"That's me," she says, not making eye contact. She already knows he'll have the same dead eyes and expressionless face as Kim. She holds out her hand and he passes over the small screen for her to sign. She scribbles her name and takes the box from him before he heads back to his van and pulls away.

With a sigh, she gets up from the steps and carries the box into her home, curious to know what's inside. She kicks her shoes off next to the door and passes Kim on the way to the kitchen. She grabs a knife from one of the drawers and runs it over the tape before throwing the utensil into the sink. She pulls back the brown cardboard and laughs when she sees the contents of the package.

OF CHAMPAGNE PROMISES
by Kim Lavoie

In addition to her advanced copy book is a small thank you note from the publisher raving about how much they loved her celebration of Kim's life and prolific career. She sets it down on the counter and flips open to the foreword she wrote and stares at the page in confusion.

I was really hoping we'd have books out at the same time again. I was really hoping we'd have books out at the same time again. I was really hoping we'd have books out at the same time again. I was really hoping we'd have books out at the same time again. I was really hoping we'd have books out at the same time again. I was really hoping we'd have books out at the same time again. I was really hoping we'd have books out at the same time again. I was really hoping we'd have books out at the same time again. I was really hoping we'd have books out at the same time again. I was really hoping we'd have books out at the same time again. I was really hoping we'd have books out at the same time again.

Feeling hysterical, Charlotte throws the book across the kitchen and hangs her head in her hands, trying to calm her breathing. Her eyes sting, her face feels hot, and all she wants is for Kim's whispering to stop.

But it doesn't stop.

It never stops.

April

Charlotte holds the book in her hands, running the tips of her fingers over the embossed cover, tracing her name on the thick paper. She should be happy, she should be filled with joy, but instead she feels... nothing. Not disappointment or sadness.

She just doesn't feel anything at all.

Kim stands across from her seat in the living room recliner, eyes wide and empty as she watches Charlotte, whispers filling the silence between them. The sound reminds her of rats in a wall scratching to get out.

She flips through the book, admiring the font and the stock of the paper. Even though her eyes scan each page, she doesn't bother trying to read anything. She knows it's pointless. The paragraphs all look the same to her now.

I was really hoping we'd have books out at the same time again. I was really hoping we'd have books out at the same time again. I was really hoping we'd have books out at the same time again. I was really hoping we'd have books out at the same time again. I was really hoping we'd have books out at the same time again...

She closes the book with a sigh, more exhausted than she's ever been in her life. She sees Kim's reflection in the glossy cover and feels the woman's eyes on her, Kim's whispering burrowing into her brain. Charlotte wants to scream, wants to cry, wants to do something, *anything,* to make the noise stop. She misses being alone in her house. It's been so long with Kim that she almost forgets what it's like not to be under constant observation.

"Happy release day, Kim," she says, looking up to stare at the other woman.

Kim looks blankly back at her.

"Let me guess," Charlotte continues, getting up from her chair and crossing the small room, "you were really hoping we'd have books out at the same time again?"

"I was really hoping we'd have books out at the same time again," she whispers.

"I thought you might feel that wa—"

"But you stole that from me."

Charlotte shivers, suddenly cold, and her heart beats faster. Although Kim has spent the last few weeks speaking at Charlotte, this is the first time she's ever spoken directly *to* her.

"What did you say?"

"You stole that from me. You stole that from *us*. Why did you hate me so much?" Kim continues, her face changing for the first time since her death. Sadness and confusion line her brow and the creases of her eyes, the corners of her mouth drawn downwards.

"I never hated you! I just—" Charlotte stops herself, throat tight. She can feel it again, the wave of grief that comes to pull her under when she least expects it.

"You just *what*?" Kim asks.

"I just wanted a chance to have what you did. I just wanted people to know my name."

Kim's expression hardens as she looks through Charlotte. "They will."

Kim advances on Charlotte, who backs away from her as quickly as her feet will carry her. Charlotte's throat begins to burn and her lungs ache as she tries to put distance between herself and Kim. She struggles to breathe, panic setting in, as Kim gets closer and closer. She coughs, trying to clear her throat. Clear liquid sputters over her lips and down her chin. It reeks of alcohol.

Kim takes another step forward and Charlotte tries to back away, but the backs of her knees hit the couch and she falls onto it.

"P-l-ease," Charlotte begs. "Puh-le-lease, Kim. I-I'm s-sor-ry."

Kim reaches out and puts a hand on her chest, pushing Charlotte down onto the couch until she's lying on her back. Charlotte kicks and flails, wanting to sit up, but she can't. The alcohol fills her mouth and burns a trail down her airway. She coughs as hard as she can, her body trying to fight as her lungs fill with liquid.

"I was really hoping we'd have books out at the same time again," Kim says with a sad smile, brushing a strand of hair off of Charlotte's forehead as she drowns.

The last thing Charlotte sees are Kim's dead eyes.

The book feels heavy in Emily's hand, and she thumbs through the pages with a heavy heart before putting it back on the display. She admires the design of the cover, the stylized art, and the sleek font of the title.

And All the Rivers Burned
by Charlotte Curran

A peach book-club sticker with a vibrant orange "O" at its centre has been fixed to each of the books. Emily can hardly believe the unexpected success that the novel has received since its publication, going so far as to make the New York Times Best Seller List in its first week of sales. She wants to believe it's because the novel is a work of art, a story that she and Charlotte believed in.

But she can't help but wonder if her former client's sudden and tragic death has helped bolster sales.

"I just... I can't help but wonder if I could have done something to help her, you know?" she says into her cellphone as she heads to the entrance of the Azure Pages.

Emily stops next to the exit, giving the store a final look before she leaves.

Charlotte stares back at her with bright eyes and a wide smile from the posters that hang from the ceiling and decorate the endcap displays.

With a sigh, Emily opens the door and heads out into the warm spring air.

Acknowledgements

Whenever someone takes a chance on my work, it's a surreal experience for me. There are always so many people I want to thank for getting me to this place in my life, but conveniently my brain forgets the full list when I try to put it down on paper, so I'm sorry if I've left anyone out!

A massive thank-you to my family for always believing in me and encouraging me to pursue my dreams. (While I still don't have a private island, I do have my name in print, so I guess I'm halfway there, dad!) Thank you to my friends, both the ones I have in-person and online, for helping me decompress whenever life gets too big (and for fueling my caffeine addiction). I really don't know what I'd do without you all. A heartfelt thank-you to my partner, who (almost) never complains when I read him the same sentence over and over again for feedback when he's in the middle of work. I love you so so much.

And, of course, an enormous thank-you to Cody at Timber Ghost Press for taking a chance on this novelette of mine. It's one of my favourite stories that I've ever written, and I really can't thank you enough for giving me a chance to share it with the world.

ABOUT THE AUTHOR

Caitlin Marceau is an author and lecturer living and working in Montreal. She holds a B.A. in Creative Writing, is a member of both the Horror Writers Association and the Quebec Writers' Federation, and spends most of her time writing horror and experimental fiction.

She's been published for journalism, poetry, as well as creative non-fiction, and has spoken about horror literature at several Canadian conventions. Her debut collection, *Palimpsest*, is available from Ghost Orchid Press and her novella, *This Is Where We Talk Things Out*, is slated for publication by DarkLit Press later this year.

If she's not covered in ink or wading through stacks of paper, you can find her ranting about issues in pop culture or nerding out over a good book.

For more information, or just to say hi, you can reach her through infocaitlinmarceau@gmail.com.

A Note from Timber Ghost Press

If you enjoyed, *Magnum Opus*, please consider leaving a review on Amazon or Goodreads. Reviews help the author and the press.

If you go to www.timberghostpress.com you can sign up for our newsletter so you can stay up-to-date on all our upcoming titles, plus you'll get informed of new horror flash fiction and poetry featured on our site monthly.

Take care and thanks for reading, *Magnum Opus* by Caitlin Marceau.

-Cody L.
Timber Ghost Press

Printed in Great Britain
by Amazon